In
Between
The bridge

by

-Abhinay Renny

Lyrics on page 66 have been taken from the song
Ennodu Nee irindhal by A.R.Rahman; on page 39
dialogue from movie, Alaipayuthey by Mani Ratnam.

Most of the characters and events in this book are
fictitious. Names, characters, places, organizations,
events and incidents are the product of the author's
imagination or are used fictitiously.

ISBN-10: 1515309363
ISBN-13: 978-1515309369

To my family and
my Basketball team

For
me and my thoughts.

CONTENTS

CONTENTS

ACKNOWLEDGMENTS

Thanks everyone for helping me to make my thought real, and specially, first and foremost,

Swathi Koduri a.k.a Celebrity !!!! Thank you so much!, If you weren't there for me, supporting me, I'd not be writing a book and acknowledging your support here.

I specially thank A.R.Rahman, for inspiring me with his music, thoughts and also Ram Gopal Varma, for his words to believe in Individuality.

Thank you! my VNR VJIET basketball family for caring me, kicking me, supporting me all the way.

Sanam Jiandani a.k.a Teddddy, Thank you so much!!! for your presence whenever I needed.

Amrutha Mynampaty, ! Thanks alot for your help, support, talks, when I'd no idea what I was upto.

I P Tharun, Thank you bro for the guidance.
I also thank Kanchana mam, for the late and best review.

I wish to acknowledge the reviews provided by Anil Raj, Amulya Gupta, Amoolya sharma, Lavanya sharma, Sameera thotapally, Sruthi Somaruthu and greeshma Raj for the translations.

Jr. Sandeep a.k.a beat boxer, thanks for the support.

Susheel! Thank you for listening my blabbering patiently and thankyou kittu krishna for the awesome front cover.

And Finally Stormy girl a.k.a Srinidhi. Thanks for everything, and time is (Check your watch).

Like a tear or a smile a poem is but
a picture of what is taking place
within.

- Rabindranath Tagore

1 THE END

Looking deep into the sky, I find masterpiece of art with a palette of colours. With apartments towering to the sky, I look at the sky sitting on the terrace of a penthouse having 15 storeys beneath it. With sun, taking the leave to shine on the other half of the world, it depicts a mix of deep reddish beaming rays amidst blue sky with white clouds displaying different shapes when seen with different perspectives.

With the cool breeze of air, caressing me, I'm lost in thoughts, thinking about the end. I look at the birds resting in sun shade on another apartment, after their end of search for the food, Old woman reading Bhagvad Gita wishing to end her life with spiritual freedom, Uncle playing candy crush while her wife crushes her angriness in mixer and irritates him, Girls grouped to gossip at the playground. 6 year child in the balcony, swiping his finger to swap the app in I pad, and kids playing beach volleyball together through Bluetooth in their smart phones.

And here I am thinking about the end.

The end of my happy times spent every evening while returning home after college with my school friends. The end of my pleasing moments with mom to go out for partying at nights, The end of being at home. The end of sneak outs, The end of landline calls. End of my plus two education gave way to engineering education, I ended up many times, thinking, "that's it, This is the end", but I saw many starts after witnessing many ends.

The End is never absolute and, always relative

Start of Engineering Education.

To start my engineering education in Hyderabad. The city of varied cultures, I've lived here for more than 3 years, starting with my 10th class till Plus two in school. It very long stays in one place in my life.

In the journey of my teen life, I have liven, learned, left and grown. And here I am starting after other end, with admission in MVR College of Engineering, Hyderabad.

I was told various opinions about branches, but at last it is me who opted the branch without getting influenced by relatives who bother to call only on my result days.

Having an elder brother who graduated, helped me to minimize all the fantasies related to the college life. He explained how it'd be in reality. When I was told about breaking the records of back log records, one night stands, gang fights, last hour preparations, ragging, scams in fests, politics, and many more. It was jaw dropping and reality seemed more interesting than fantasy. Yeah, May be, My reality could be fantasy to someone.

Two things I want to make clear in my choice of Engineering,

I joined engineering by choice, I want to study engineering course, so that 4 years will give ample time to think about, who I really am. Time to search for what I am among the bunch of people striving with many aspirations, ideas, thoughts, philosophies to make their dreams real, to realize their dreams. If I end up with thought, at the last year of my engineering, mechanical engineer. If my childhood's one day dream is what I really wanted to become on that day, then I'd be on the right path.

I joined Engineering to explore, besides getting a certificate in "Mechanical Engineering".

Anything which is mainstream is odd.Learning how to laugh while you cry, seems more interesting than learning, laughing at laughing classes at morning 6am. I chose engineering too, to learn every other possible thing, besides learning Engineering.

With so many ends, I had equal starts, giving a ray of hope for a better tomorrow. I never care about start until I reach the end.

First day of my college.

Where are beautiful girls in this college?!!!!!. As speaker failed to have my attention in a formal induction program meant for boasting. With fear, with anxiety, I wander in college, in search of beautiful girls. In fear, with false coolness on my face, I take a stroll around the buildings, I look at the board, hung from the ceiling by chains, named MECHANICAL ENGINEERING DEPARTMENT.

I smile and look at the campus from my block, 3rd floor. I look at the long road, all buildings are placed aside and labs on either side. I look at gang of 20, gearing up for the ride, couple creating their own world, nerds running behind lecturers, girls going out, acknowledging their fans following. I see guy with head- sets over his ears sitting on bench, writing so seriously, and I see couple pacing towards administrative building. College ambience is so perfect, to grow up as person, to live as a friend, to work as a student, to love as a lover, College is everything needed to let the student shape his personality and strive to know himself.

After looking at college, I started to hostel where I have to live for four years, I imagined a big building block cornered from the circuited girls hostel with a series of rooms filled with stenched clothes, blowing air instead of running water in the taps. I am struck dumb standing in front of a large gates of gated community where my hostel lies. My college doesn't own a hostel!!!. They leased villas to provide hostels. Seniors and juniors in separate gated communities. I entered into gated community looking at large number of duplex villas complexioned in cream colour, covered with a canopy of trees. Floodlights at ends to lighten up the whole lanes. I enter my allotted villa, consisting 3 spacious bedrooms, common hall, common kitchen. I smile, saying, "God blessed my college".

I'm the first hostler reporting on 1st day of college. Alone in a whole big villa, I go to terrace and spend the evening travelling back to my past. I sit at the End of the Terrace, sliding my legs to the air hanging and travel back thinking about the places I've travelled.

Travelling back!

I did my schooling in 9 different schools, 9 different places. If there is any reason to be proud about my schooling life, it is about the number of schools I've studied in. Looking at perks of getting transfer every year, one can travel a lot. My father is Govt employee who gets transferred frequently and I love it. I have studied each class in a different school, different place. I studied more in the school of hard knocks than in my formal education. At first, I found difficult to find friends. As time passed by, I've learned to make friends in the nick of time and also leave the place at the eleventh hour. But I have made friends who still are with me whenever I need. I talk to them once in a blue moon, but whenever I talk, I feel so close to them and share each and everything happened in my life. I remember and recollect the memories at the drop of a hat.

Unlike Abraham Lincoln, who wrote a letter to his son's teacher, my father never even talked to one of my school teachers. He doesn't bother to know how I'm doing with my studies, he visits school only two times for two reasons. For admission at start of the school and for certificates at end of the school. Having no one who really cares about my education, I ended up being an average student till primary school.

Once In my 8th class, with very bad performance in term examination, I got "D" grade. With so much sadness and fear, I went near my father with my report card, he signs with an expressionless face and before I leave with shame, he calls me and ask, "Do you know, why you got less marks ?". With stammering voice I answered, "I didn't study well". He takes me for a walk and says, "I'm glad you know the reason for your bad performance, from now on it's you, who is responsible for your work, decisions". "No one is going to live up for you, you need to take care of yourselves and your decisions." Though It seemed preaching, a walk with my dad on a cloudy evening raised the curtain for the upgrade of "Excuse master 8.0" I stopped giving excuses and took everything that came on my way.

Travelling taught me to have my own school of thought. I have a special affinity to notorious personalities than famous heroes. Hitler, Veerappan, Osama Bin laden, Saddam Husain, Ram Gopal Varma .... I was not influenced by their school of thought, but got surprised to know the reasons that made them to live in that particular, "school of thought". I grew up listening A.R.Rahman's mellowing melodies, living far away from hometown, I grew up realizing "home is where the heart is". I've lived in bungaloid suburbs, I've also lived in bustling areas. I've travelled to places looking at so many people and pondered whether people work to worry or be worried to work. I saw many parents spending lakhs for a lucrative business, crores for costly buildings. I also saw parents struggling to send their children to school, striving to satisfy kids' needs. I saw waterfalls, I also saw places where water drop never falls, I sat with people who lived in poverty, I also sat with people who lived with loads of properties. I saw the region influence over religion, I also saw a legion living for the region. I found places packed nuts to butts with banging crowd, I also found a serene place while I snuck out. I read books, but I'm not a book worm, I party hard, but not a party animal. I'm **Karthick** with 'c' in between I and K, leaving my home for the first time.

I share my room with two people, Sanjay, Aditya. Three first time hostlers in same room. Unlike me, they come with their caring parents telling them to take care four times in a minute. I wish my dad at least could have dropped me in the hostel, leave me saying a few words. *He already said alot*, "Your life, your responsibility, take care". I talk with their parents and answer all the formal questions they posed. Sanjay comes from Nellore and Aditya from Warangal. Both are gadget geeks, always wired to either tab or phone. We spent the night talking about girls, games, college and at last had to talk about gadgets also.

Started to college with excitement. With beautiful senior sitting in front, ragging you sweetly, what more on earth is called happiness?

I don't want any other senior to eye on me and rag.
I'm happy, I am being ragged by 4th year senior
named Sruthi, like her sweet name she is also
sweet.

Then there comes her gang, full of guys and girls
rounding me. Being scared, I expressed my fear
with stammered voice, I was asked to tell my bio
data in many languages while I run through
invisible hurdles, revolve round the pole, ride on
the rocket. Luckily, all the lady seniors ragged me
sweetly, Sweet girls really can't rag! They call a
random fresher girl to sit beside me and ask me to
write love letter to her.

I write,

Dear "fresher girl",

*Not until I
saw you, I had a heart with
throb, throbbing me to be
with you, spend my life with*

you, Will you be my love?
Will you be my life being
with me. I take leave, letting
you know, I'll woo you,
sweep off your feet with my
love and make your life
meaningful with me.

Karthick
Karthick10695@gmail.com

Nothing on the letter is real except the feelings which are for my love, whom I've wanted to meet since the time I left my primary school.

Though everyone got impressed with the letter, With a serious expression on the face, they made me to play basketball without ball, play guitar without it.

I receive a request from my first love letter recipient. In urge of increasing the social status;

virtual like the site, I accepted and found her boring.

HOSTELS ,GROUPS, COLLEGE.

With lines, " we screw so hard that even metals cry", Groups are made on Whatsapp, Facebook. socializing to screw time. With the flood of friend requests, likes, comments, my Facebook notifications reached 250 on one day itself. I started searching for the one who can talk freely on face and also Facebook.

       Social site is helping to socialize virtually, but not really. Being conversation maker, I easily socialized with many friends who ought to be best buddies, 3am friends in future. I met Raul, the footballer. I was shocked after meeting Suhas the baller, hostler since his kindergarten, knows nothing perfectly except English. Suveen, the lost. Sunil, Shyam. I've met many and became friends. With equal excitement on faces, we mingled so easily and formed gang of 13. Very soon we became really close, partying together, bunking together. Of all, Raul is the first person to be taken and get ECE chick, Ramya . Excluding him, the rest of us with rugged faces, enjoyed our own time with no girls to love, no girls to care, no tension to suffer.

Being in a hostel is fun, Being in Villas with friends, without anyone to say, "No" for anything , is still more fun. Loving the times spent in hostel, As soon as I come out of college freed from seniors, ragging, I spend the rest of the time with friends talking Endlessly. Time flied by Late night walks, Movie screenings, Lan gamings.

After losing the fear every 1st year fresher has on his 1st day. We started bunking. we started exploring the college, College with many buildings is too good to bunk. We can kill time by sleeping in Future vision centre, after a sleepless night spent in hostel. These Future vision centres are home theatre rooms allotted to screen all Engineering documentaries, What a privilege to sit and relax. We found library, the noisiest place with seniors smooching round the corners. we found ground, the silent place, with no one playing. Students are meant to break the silence, we started playing and here we are daily after classes playing, while other freshers are busy flattering girls who have pretty faces.

Mobbing all around like bosses, we were called as hard core idiots. Everyone in the gang is so special in their own style. Like every class has every personality, we also had many. Being so diverse, we still stayed together roaming in college to kill time rather than attending boring lectures. It all seemed stereotyped, when I looked at beautiful seniors roaming among us, While we are behind our gorgeous English mam, greeting her "good morning".

In the midst of all the buzz of Fresher's excitement, My excitement was so vulnerable like fossil fuel, I lost it very easily. Nothing new happened in college within new days of my college life. I'm feeling so bored. Being idle all the time paved way for a thought of trying a new adventure, new exploration. Though I'm not sure about what I think right now, I decided to do something to beat the boredom. I walk outside of my gated community. Standing out at the gates, I look around the place. To get away from the bustle of busy people, I head to high way with no money, no phone.

Being in the corner of the city, I walk towards the outer ring road, in search of some mysterious place at eventide. I slowly get on to the Outer ring road through a broken mesh of wires. With a gush of huge trucks, I decided to mount the rock which stands next to the snake shaped road. With dimmed light beamed by the sun, I get onto the rock slowly, carefully and reach the top. The rock spread with green trees, bushes, eroded slant land, and huge stones. I sit at the tip of the rock looking at dark black road lit with lights of vehicles and city embellished with lights, stars and moon aggrandizing the dark sky. I look up at the sky wondering what is this space made up of? . Lines run through my mind expressing the moment.

Mountain has its charm to please me
Heights are where, triggers a thought

Sat in cold place
to know beauty of space

Vehemently floating amongst fantasized clouds
Incessantly drowning into reality river

Universe is clever
to stifle the beauty
Man as ever
discovering new, as a duty

Sky full of stars
Yet, dull at city

Colours endearing the heart
Rovers gearing up to cover naut

Unveiling the space
from living place
To show new way to our race.

Clear sky cleanses my heart, mind with no
thoughts. I feel serene being here. The Adventure
turned out to be a treasure hunt where I found my
treasure, calmness, peace. When I was idle, I had no
thoughts, Even after sitting on this rock, I'm having
no thoughts. But the only difference is calmness in
my mind, freshness in my heart.

Now, I'm all rejuvenated to find something new,
creative, in the newdays of my college life.

Heading to the hostel, I'm all around my well
wishers wishing me to pursue my dreams.
Encouraging me to strive for what I want to
become.

Having interest to play basketball, I go near people who seemed like college players and asked if I can join them. I had my piece of cake, I got ragged and then after being asked about my presence on court, I explained them about my interest. Looking at me, they ordered me to show my rugged face on the court at 4. I got ragged by mechanical seniors who seemed bossy, Raghu bhai and Sai bhai.

I'm the only first year who is attending the practice and it is team practice. I walk to the ring and Start collecting rebounds and then pass it to the seniors. I looked at the team of 12 slowly making their appearance on court. Generally Basketball captain is the one who has many girl followers, I was searching for the "captain celebrity" , I was asked about my details by a man who is short, fair with good physique, he came with mop cleaning the court and I told my bio data which I repeated 203+ times in Telugu, English, Hindi.

Raghu bhai introduces him as captain, "Teja Bhai". Looking at him, I was utterly shocked. I expected 6footer with gym body being centre of attraction, but here I see captain cleaning the court. Humble

person. With severe shock, I lined up with the team
and started practice

O captain, My captain.

With Teja Bhai's call, I joined the team to run 4km
to warm up, to start the practice. With another
shock, I dared to run 4km and stopped half way,
holding my stomach panting badly. I get a push
from back ordering me to run, I slowly pulled up
till warm up and witnessed the hard core practice,
I ever saw in my life. Ball handling drills, German
drills, sprints, what not!

After a week of hard core practice, I was witnessing
the team who plays to win, but not plays to
participate. Champion team of Hyderabad
engineering colleges since the beginning. We walk,
we run, we jump, we crawl, we do everything on
court sweating all over the body.

When I pass the ball in wrong manner. Captain
comes with a wicked smile and shouts, "God damn
mother fucker, get your butt out of court and run 4
rounds around it". Everyone of us follows without
raising our voice. We are always set with limit
which is beyond our capacity, we pushed our limits

every day, in every way becoming better day by day
and become strong mentally, physically.
With every slang spoken on court by the captain, he
pushes us to do better every day, his words inspire
us, his presence makes us to suspire after heavy
drills, his every word makes us to question our self
about our play.

No matter what happens, we all practiced every day
and during the tournaments time, it's hard core hell
practice. After practicing so hard for tournaments,
I've attended my first tournament in IMED college.

Imagining to witness the awesome game, I look at
Teja Bhai sprinting on the court talking to move the
center forward to screen for side forward. With art
of distraction, he passes the ball to low post swiftly
and assist for the basket. After a cake walk of
league rounds, I witnessed the worst ankle twist of
Raghu Bhai in semifinals!. He still plays the finals,
with the mind boggling defense, he helps the team.
We win the finals and the crowd appreciates with
standing ovations.
Everyone is heroes at their home, but gaining the
away crowd appreciation, caused the stir.

Raghu trudged with pain taking other's support,

When he was asked "Why you played with so much of struggle"

"Everyone wants it, but all it matters is How badly you want?"

Teja calls Raghu, 6footer," Chotu, girl at the corner is staring at you, What say? Go, talk!"

And they walked away with a smile, pride on their faces for the win.

I sit on my villa terrace, with my diary, writing

Date/year/
                  Raghu Bhai words are so encouraging
and inspiring, all he believes in is, effort. Effort to
the fullest is what he regards as WIN. No wonder,
he is a great player.

If I win, I win,
Lose, If I lose
It's not the result, I see
The try, to the FULLEST
is what I mean
"The wIn"

Contented with the comfort, happiness with huddle made in the ground. I wish to see more happiness, craziness in most dumbest, boring things in my life. Worried about why I'm not worried for the final exams. Hope I write my exams happily without any hustle in my mind.

I smile sitting on the terrace with the diary. I look at the beautiful blue diary stolen from my dad. And hop down through the staircase with my diary, guitar and reach my room.

27 missed calls on my phone screen!

I was deadly scared. I envisaged dad's serious lecture on carelessness, mom's mugged up scoldings, but no. To my surprise, Santosh, friend from my 10th class called. After reading his message, it was about night out. He asked me if I could join. I have an exam tomorrow, my first B.tech, first semester examination. I gave a deep thought. I texted, " yes, pick me up at my place, I'm coming". On shorts, with my books, I got into the car and reached his home. We started to the farm house and reached a beautiful place 40km away from the city. I got down and stretched myself

looking at the beautiful place, seemed corner of
the village. I was welcomed with barks of "Boxer
breed" dogs frightening me, scaring me.

With a mix of emotions, I enter
the farm house, looking at the big swimming pool,
barking dogs, green lawns, spacious triplex building,
I was left in thought that farm house is for sure
going to fuck up my exams.

With loud trance music, spacious space around us,
we shook our heads and waved our hands and
jumped over the couch. Looking at big, blue
watered pool outside, We brought the loud
speakers out of the house. We dove into the water,
playing water volleyball and enjoyed swimming. At
night, I was not only, "the one in the gang" who
drank maaza while others had beer. Few friends
accompanied me.

At midnight, 4 of us, sober heads headed for the
city to get some more alcohol for drunkards in the
house. While my friend hit the gas pedal, we reach
city within 40 minutes. Under the bright street
lights on the road, in a trice we are overtaken by
whizzing SUV drifted to side of the road and hits
the divider making our jaws drop. We look at the
vehicle hitting the divider. We are dead scared to go

near. None of us got down from the car. We looked at the SUV with shocks on our faces, trying to realize that whatever happened is real. Thanks to advanced safety technology, no one got killed. Everyone in the car simply walked away talking among themselves about an insurance claim. They leave before cops book them under "drunk and drive".

With shocking faces, we head back to the farm house with a case of beers and memories of school life. We are on a deserted road, driving with snail speed and talking about past times. I rest my face on the window looking at the dark night and suddenly start typing on my phone.

I am happy
Being in "Good old times"

I am happy
With 7 more hours to hell

I am happy
with loss of lazy cops

Heading home
To halt, to hurry

**For the exams
With a worry**

**For the missing feeling
Called "FEAR".**

Reaching home at the crack of dawn, we planned to play cricket enjoying the weather. Though we are exhausted, we never wanted to fall in bed to sleep. With strained eyes deprived of sleep, we jumped into chilled cool watered pool after the hard play. When clock struck 9, I start hurriedly to the city in car with my friend. I wish, I had more worry about the exam than worry about morning traffic. I finally reached college with heavy eyes.

Decided to try on luck for 1st exam, English exam. I look at my friend to say "bye" but, he revved the engine and vanished out of my sight. Before I enter into college I checked out what I need to carry for the exam, hall ticket, identity card, pen. I see everyone giving me weird looks. Before I realize that I'm in shorts, The clock struck 10!! exam time!!. I rushed into examination hall showing id card and hall ticket, whoever obstructed my way.

Besides giving question paper, the examiner gave pathetic looks. I silently scolded my friend for not reminding me to wear pants. He vanished intentionally to make me feel awkward that situation. After some time, feeling free with shorts, I ignored other looks and started filling up the answer sheets. With weird start on 1st exam, finished all exams with one night preparation and wrote all other exams well, but not in shorts!!!!!!

1 THE START

End of 1st year gave way to "senior", 2nd year of engineering, yet I can't find, what I really want to become. I Spent time by sleeping, playing, exploring, dreaming.

Reading Socrates quote stuck in my room,

"The beginning of wisdom is the definition of terms."

With so many swaying thoughts in my mind, I write in my journal.

"DREAM" is a journey,
Portraying subconscious plot

"TO DREAM" is a journey of
Picturing the person's passion.

"LOVE" is a journey
Loving others as yourself

"TO LOVE" is a journey of
Give, forgive and live.

After writing about a dream, to dream and love, to love, I am in dream ,dreaming about love, loving someone.

LOVE. Like air on earth, silence in space, ocean in drop, there is one feeling which connects everyone in this world with magical enigma chaining everyone's heart. If I start my day reasoning on sunshine on earth, snowfall on home, cry of a just born baby, exuberance of a child, brother's care for young, Blush of a wife, dad's scoldings, pampering the daughter, moan of mellowed lady while sex, cuddle of aged couple, smile on each and everyone's face.

I conclude for the existence of feeling, "LOVE" to cease you, ease you through times, while every ray beams on earth from the sun.

I was in love, I was overwhelmed with love, but, never loved. I quote on love , "love others as yourself". I couldn't love anyone like how I love myself. Probably not until I meet someone who'll be my life.

The only cool, easy going year without any worry or
fear is the 2nd year of engineering. Plenty of time for
not to think about future plans, plenty of time to
waste it as nothing can teach us the value of time for
now. Plenty of time to enjoy the freedom of
seniority. In all the fuss of seniors ragging juniors. I
met so many of my batch mates whom I never saw in
college. After becoming seniors, everyone became
busy ragging juniors, making them to write the
records, assignments.

The Meet

I enter into the canteen filled up with couples
cornering themselves, having an endless talk, a group
of juniors being ragged ruthlessly by my classmates.
With clatter of spoons and plates, screeching noise of
the fans. With dim light falling onto the tables, I was
exhorted to pick up Raul for the party from his
girlfriend's gang. Out of everyone in the gang, Girl
with big eyes, peace complexioned face and dimple
on cheek while she is smiling subtly, set her loose
black hair with curls at end and with all cuteness in
her, she grabbed my attention. She is sitting there as
an observer in the group of people, listening to
endless giggles, discussions done in the gang.
Her eyes magnetized me, making my eyes fix on her.
Being a conversation maker, I stood there speechless

28

being stuck, looking at her, standing opposite to her, staring at her.

I looked at the beautiful big eyes. I was frigged when she moved the fringes. I was stunned looking at her charming face. She is a girl who can turn heads. Like line tracer bot, I traced her eyes, moving my eyes wherever she moves. With calm expressions, she observes what others are talking. I pinch Raul to introduce me and I am introduced as "Karthick" stressing the letter 'c'. While Raul introduce all the circuited geeks names, Ignoring all the boring names, I was elated listening to her name, "Amrutha "; nectar to my life.

The Next day, I drag Raul to accompany me to the canteen. Letting him sit with his girlfriend, Ramya. I search for the sweet nectar in the group. She sits in a corner being an observer in the boasting gang. I look at her in the group, while everyone is busy blabbering. I pretended to be normal, not expressing my excitement on face, I wish her through a smile and she smiles at me.

As there is a notion of invisibility of EEE Department students in college, I tried searching for her next few days. I couldn't find her in the mob, in the class. Time flied. I start the day thinking about her, I end the night thinking about her. She became the mess in my mind, messing my memory with her mesmerizing eyes.

After 20 days

While I was hogging after heavy practice at 6.40, someone taps my shoulder to call me. I was surprised by Amrutha's presence and wished her heartily with a smile. She stood behind me with a bag, hanging on one side. Her big merry eyes talk a lot than her soft red lips with pulp of orange on them, she carries pulpy orange in one hand and set her tousled hair stroking it back. She looks elegant in her perfect slender body, wearing a sumptuous blue top and black denim. She wears no gold, which can look dull by her face glow. Setting her tousled hair now and then she looks so perfectly stunning. The way she is carrying herself so fabulously, made me to be in her trance. With her Mellifluous voice, she says

" hi.... Hmm, I 'd like to know if there are any buses to Madura Nagar". With awe I nod at her, showing my bus to travel half the way home.

There are no Madura Nagar buses, Despite of her bus arrival within 35 minutes. I acted selfishly to travel with her. I escort her till bus. She sits at window side with hurried expression on her face to reach home early. Being gentle, I didn't make conversation for the first time with the girl who stunned me with her surprised presence.

I was wished with cute smile, with dimple on her cheek. I am not exaggerating things happened between us, but absolutely happy. I'm so happy, where I didn't want to express it with status on social site, but write some lines in my diary to cherish the moments.

I write

Heart of clatter is calm, smiling
Surprising myself with melody mellowing me.
Loving the little things left with me
To meet, To greet.

Her headphones fell down while she got down from the bus, I took them looking at her, crossing the road with scarf showing only those big gleaming kohl treated black eyes. Looking at the headphones, I reach my hostel refreshing myself. I sit in my room looking at the headphones, JBL J56BT. Listening Shreya ghosal's Saans seemed listening my heart throb Amrutha's magical voice in audio cancellation mode, nothing except her voice enthralled me, while I sit in my room and roam in green pastures. I'm mad!!!! I'm hallucinating her voice.

People are so mad to see god in stone, I see special warmths even in headphones, after all, we are humans, creators of creator of creation.

Next day. Amrutha being behind me with pulpy orange in one hand. I wish her with smile and walk towards bus. I gave her headphones. I am not afraid to make a conversation with her, but I don't want to scare her, with my blabbering, hammering about whatever comes to mind. To say, Nothing except herself is in my mind.

I enjoy travelling with her daily, I'm enjoying, being with her. I love this happy hours of my life living in this moment, not expecting anything from her, except her presence and smile. After fortnights of fervid fever of excitement, enticement, I was sad with a broken heart with arrival of Madura Nagar bus before time. I'm sure she'll get onto that bus. She'd know about my lie on "no Madura Nagar buses". I can't travel with her anymore. I stood still while both the buses arrive.

I walk towards my bus, thinking she'd go on another bus.

I am bewildered. She gets onto my bus following me. And sit in front me, looking at me with a teasing smile. I am still in bewilderment and gave awkward

32

smile. I can't understand the expressions on such a beautiful face. I sit silently, looking at window, ignoring others while I act as if I'm ignoring her expressions, gaze towards me. She sets her tousled hair, sitting cross legged in an opulent dark green kurthi with dimple on her cheek, when she smiled.

I broke the silence after small conversation we make every day with smiles, "why did you get onto this bus, Madura Nagar bus is next to it."

All she said, with a smile is, " I know".

I was so perplexed with the answer, "I know" (with teasing smile) .When a girl   says   something,

They can be so deep, deeper than the oceans. Indeterminable deepest lines are spoken by girls. With no confidence, I asked "when did you know?"

" The day after you told me, 'no Madura Nagar buses'", offering me headphones to listen her music. She could see the shock in my face, sitting beside her, I listen to Latha Mangeshkar's "Aaj Kal Paon". LathaMangeshkar's magical voice didn't stimulate me, but amrutha's minute mixed expressions on her face took me to the edge of my seat. What does she think now??? A million dollar question!!!.

I didn't dare to attack her with loads of questions, running in my mind.

Does she like my company? Does she know, I'm affine to her? Should I convey? Is she the one who can make me shine?

Sun shines, rain falls, snow comes, there are a couple of people, with whom I want to spend quality time sharing my thoughts, love.

Amrutha and my Basketball team.

Days spent together travelling in same bus, we shared our music choices, books, thoughts, love on nature, beaches, brimmed milkshake with creams, we feel complete with each other's company. And I got to know so many startling things about her,

She is Amrutha!!. With Malayali mother, Tamilian father, she finished her schooling in place called Dharwad; Kannada daughter. Till now I managed in English, but to get into her family and talk with her family members, I need to learn Malayalam, 3rd toughest language in the world, Tamil, and to express and impress, Kannada. Hell may break loose.

Amrutha is a vocalist and also a violin player in our college band. She daily stays late for jamming sessions and travel with me. As soon as I'm done with practice, I look behind, looking for her arrival. She saunters with pulpy orange in one hand and bag in the other hand.

Call it for any day, she won't be without pulpy orange in her hand.

Malayalis love coconuts, Tamilians love sambar, kannada loves baath. This 3state girl loves "Pulpy orange". Amu's presence makes me bliss, I'm so happy with whatever is happening, I love this moment, love the subtle conversation we make with eyes every day. Being a big blabberer, I choose to stay calm in her presence, not with fear but with enamour. My day doesn't end without the wish of Amu.

Time flied. Karthick and Amrutha felt incomplete without each other. Amrutha waits for Karthick after jamming session. Karthick does the same if she doesn't appear without her pulpy orange. A travel of 25 minutes every day, is what both craved for.

Karthick, in his room with many pensive thoughts.

Both of us are comfortable with each other's presence and I get this serene feeling with her around me. I feel, she is the girl who can make me cry, smile, laugh, shine, grow and live for the life with meaning which has to be explored.

I finally gave a call to myself to express my feelings.
When the genuine feeling is expressed, it doesn't need
any special form to impress. The genuiness is the
jewel of the feeling to feel it.

I write words from my heart, asking her if she knows
what I am and what she is, to me.

After practice, I walk to jam room with bells on,
asking for a walk. We are walking on long road
called,' Lords pitch' of our college with no one at
sight. Amrutha is impeccably dressed in dazzling
black kurthi - never a hair out of place. With love on
my nerves, I feel so high. With bit nervousness, high
spirits, I stop and look into her eyes, saying,

"
I'm lost in you without being with you,

I'm loving you without trying you!,

I want you to be in my life, living with me, loving me.

I ask you all this because

if you like me,

I'd like to live with you, and love you ".

I give the rose and handmade heart shaped card with words written, and look at her with a smile. She opens the petaly noir fragranced card, looking at inked words.

Do you know
I am not a wanna be
Do you know
I want to be whom you wanna see
Do you know
You are queen to me
Do you know
You are rare to see.

She smiles.
Looking into my eyes, "ennaku teriyu[1]", she said.

Saying it, she drinks her pulpy orange and offers to me for the first ever time after meeting her daily for more than a month.

Girls!!, Girl's words are complicated than the complex enigma code. No cipher can compete in complexing encryption of hidden meaning. Hours spent on watching all the Malayalam, Tamil, Kannada

---

[1]In tamil: I know

movies didn't go in vain. I understood the word meaning, but not, what she really mean by that.

"Amrutha, Will you be the nectar of my life?"

"Sometimes I'm bitter too" She said, with subtle smile, holding her hands on hip.

I ask her seriously and she is messing with me!!. I ask her straight away with whatever Tamil, I learnt watching Thalaivar , Dhanush, Surya movies.

" Naa unnai love panraein, Vunnaku naan pudicha[2]??".

She looked around, after seeing no one in sight, she came close to my ear and whispered, "I'll be your nectar of life and you are mine!".

I stood there stunned by her reply and looked at her Malayali merry eyes. I hugged her taking into my arms, she became my teddy bear, slender, svelte, sexy teddy bear.

We walked till gate, talking to each other.

---

[2] I love you, Do you like me?

"What made you take this much long time dumbo?? ", she asked.

"I was busy in learning Tamil dialogues to propose you,

Amrutha! naan unna virumbala un maela aasai padla, nee azhagaa irukkannu nenakkala, aana, adhudhaan nadandhudumonnu bayama irukku!"

I said memorizing Maniratnam's magic words from Alaipayuthey.

She halts and said, "Maniratnam magic can't workout everywhere. Did you write anything on any girl?"

"No, No girl swept my feet, No girl moved my heart"

"From now on, no one will, except me", she said.

"I used to write about what I love. Then nature, now, chellam kutty", I hold her looking into eyes, in which I can see the space, cross the galaxies, live eternally. Beautiful big merry eyes. Her eyes do the magic making me fall for her, everytime I look at them.

Even the wiry body will also end with wrinkles, but eyes don't change. God blessed the beautiful sparkling eyes!!!

" I love writing poems on your eyes "

"I love reading your words about me". She said.

I'm sure this reader will love the writer and his writings.

"Ninna manassininda helu. Mounadallu ninna Preetiyannu arthamaadikollaballe."

I was confused with all different soundings, after requesting to repeat the lines again, she writes it on paper and asks to help myself out, with a crumble of words. With the terrible help from Google translator I am laughing, shouting while reading it.

I jumped with joy, taking the letter with me. I got out of the room, looking at the sky and everything seemed beautiful. Quivering leaves, birds perching on tree, I could only see hearts in the sky painted with white foam on the light blue sky. I dance with the letter and comfort myself in the room, thinking how I'd fast forward the time to the next evening to meet my secret of energy, not boost, but my baby. I stare at the clock and. Every move by seconds hand seemed to move at snail speed teaching me patience to wait. I sit out in the balcony waiting till the sun replaces moon, till stars stop sparkling in surrealistic sky.

Next Day.

After a hot shower, I get into room with towel,
seeing my girl Amrutha on my bed, in my room, in
my villa, in my gated community!!

"What are you doing in my hostel?"

"I'm living with you, live in relationship is trending
now, I want to be with you, so here I am."

"Stop the prank", I go near her on a towel with wet
hair. She pushes me to go get dressed. After getting
dressed, she hugs me telling, "Sweet pie, I'm moving
into your hostel for a month!!!!"

After being in relationships, lovers lack important
quality, TIME MANAGEMENT. Most lovers crave
for spending time together, the world has listened to
us.

With sudden special tours of amrutha's mom and dad.
They are leaving her at the hostel for a month. She is
going to stay with me for one month. Day, night,
Morning, Evening.

She quickly hugs me, telling, "I'll join you tomorrow,
amma, appa are waiting, I'll leave byeeee. "

I left for college practice and return.

Nothing can bring me, more happiness than Amu's stay in hostel. She'd stay for day or two in her allotted villa, but she's going to change into my room. I'm glad, I'm no more fresher to share room with other people. I started fantasizing about our stay in the same room for all the day and night. Interrupting my fantasies, Amrutha called and said,

"What if I wish to stay with you for one month in your room, being with you, sleeping with you?"

With so much of excitement, I said, "Always welcome, I'll make my room neat, cozy, for you my love."

She has already put conditions saying, we should not work on practicals of Indian taboo word 'sex'.

I nodded for her word, " what's more hurry, such a long life, I'd really love to lose virginity on a night at the beach than in my stinky room."

As soon as I reached the room after practice, She moved into my room. She cleaned the room and made it so neat and beautiful. I hugged and lifted her saying, " Amu kutty, I love you".

After completing the dinner, we cuddled up in my

cozy bed making us warm till the stars faded out.

We spent 4 beautiful days and nights in the same room sharing everything. Making every night so memorable with our talks, writings, readings. Nothing more, I can expect a happy start in my relation than this. Before I look forward to share the bliss for more days, her distant cousins from Rameshwaram reached Hyderabad and her parents insisted that she returned home.

With so much of happiness for the 4 days we spent. We spent the last night on the terrace, looking at the stars and the moon, while I strum my gutiar singing song , "Abhi na jao chod kar", asking her not to leave me. Before I finish the lines, "ke dil abhi bhara nahin", she kisses me four times for the beautiful four days we spent together.

 "4 days has 96 hours"

"4 days has 5760 minutes, so?"

"Make the magic number count"

"4 is our magic number silly sweet pie, chalo, look at my scorpion star, shining brightly."

She hugs me tightly tendering her love, affection and we spent the day cuddling each other until earth sails from west to east to depart us for the moment.

❖

In between the bridge of time, spent with lover and friends. I acknowledged the fact that, on an average one can lose two best friends after being taken. Priorities have changed. Besides, with Amrutha, the only friend I spend quality time with,   is   Suhas, my best friend, my teammate.

Being in practice, I spend quality time with him and I feel bad for his family's belief in superstitions.

✓

Takes on Trains

Unlike traditional style of wearing saffron clothes with all the beard, this person is smart, dignified, wearing lee cooper jeans, puma t shirt and with radiance in his face, sitting on couch casually. He was preaching in Suhas home. Before Suhas leave his home with huge backpack.

Babaji smiled.

He wished Suhas, "happy journey, you'll face problems in this trip, take care".

Suhas told me, about Babaji and his foretelling.

"Did your Baba tell about 'the best friend', who helps you during hard times". I asked, teasing him.

"Yes", he said.

"The least in the world I bother about, is you and your Baba", I said.

And here I am, in train wondering how Babaji forecasted this difficulty. Universe is mystery and even people who are in it.

4.40 pm DD/MM/YYYY

I'm lost in thoughts.

Like a cake walk, we reached finals, we won all the league rounds and stepped into finals. As a team, we know how many evenings we spent sweating on court to make this happen. Everyone are preparing themselves for this, except six footer.

He is in the thought process of how to convey it to the team.

First chance of playing for the universities, 54minutes to board the train and to move towards Bhubhaneshwar, and his dreams.

Rathod bhai, the captain started telling, "Suhas!, you'll play low post and box out Rony, make sure, he doesn't get any rebounds".

Looking at the expressionless face , "Don't worry bro, we'll make you fly as soon as we are done with this, we won't let you miss the universities", He told.

As captain had started telling the plays, he was convinced about their decision on him, for the finals.

When Suhas still had 27 minutes to catch the train, 7 minutes of 2nd quarter has ended, we are 4 points down, I pat Suhas telling "make it count boy, convert the free throws".

Many rebounds, many post moves, still got defeated with 2 points, and now I see why each free throw is as precious as scoring in offense, we lost. Shook hand to all the opponents wishing them congratulations. Before the flood of final winner's selfies come, we left the court and sat in a shady place with all silence in the team.

8 minutes still left on Loco pilot's watch to rev the engine and start, and same 8 minutes are left on Suhas watch for the alarm to remind his happy journey for university games. Though I'm studying mechanical engineering, never had any fantasy

towards cars, bikes. Now I love to make one, and ride floating bike, just to avoid the havoc, Hyderabad traffic.

He missed the train and here I am, looking at his expression less face with thousand thoughts running in his mind, we are at one corner of the city, 1 hour to reach railway station and with blessings of traffic, 3 hours may be. Captain revved the engine and drove hell for leather towards railway station. He drove with so much of speed that he was greeted by slangs with so many well wishers on road who got overtaken by us.

If there was any meeting held at railway station, it was us! we are on the 10th platform discussing for 3 minutes about probability of boarding train which is on 1st platform. With irritation of probabilities of success and failure, I decided to start working than sulking, Double the irritation I had, I saw in ticket issuer's face, as he feels, issuing a ticket is carving Ellora idols. I wish this person get paid for each and every time he smiles and works cordially with people, ussh!! money can really make many things,

We always ran to beat each other on grounds, but never at railway station, to get on to the train. Panting heavily, we got on to the train and as people boast about anti corruption with #no_bribe . We ignored every status update with no bribe hash tag by us and started bribing ticket collector. Any job designated as collector is always hand full of cash, call for ticket collector or bill collector. Satisfied ticket collector gave us berth to sit down.

People on train stared at us. We looked at ourselves with shabby shorts, muddy flip flops, sweaty shirts and no wonder we received such a nice welcome from co passengers. We bribed collector in a nice way, he even entertained us with his company, "money makes many things", actually I bribed, Suhas doesn't know Telugu, and also how to talk to people to get things done.

Never mind how smelly railway toilets are, I tolerated it, just to stand by to charge phones. During childhood, children used to cry for window seat, now for the electric plug socket. I look at the city of lights, passing very quickly wishing me a good journey, I'm lost in my looping thoughts similar to the rhythm of train sound.

22.00 DD/MM/YYYY (clock still ticking)

Still two more hours to reach Vijayawada. And have to reach Vizag before 6.40 am and board Ap Visaka express. It reaches there by 7.00 am and with immense confidence on Indian railway timings, with so much of relaxation and confident guess, I know it won't reach before 7.17 am.

" Suhas!, we made it bro", I said.

"Never on earth, I wish to get on to the train without charging my phone, this train sucks dude" He laughed.

"How many times did you board train?"

"May be 3 or 4, and first time in sleeper",

"Filthy rich bastard", I smiled.

I started blabbering on very random things and he sadly had to put up with me till this journey ends.

Though Amrutha had fought with me last night, she woke me up at 12'o clock saying sorry. I don't understand, when girls will get upset or moody. Understanding the situation, Without posing many questions, she urged to be safe and return safe. I smile and say, "Aama, seri".

"Girls! I say", said Suhas with wide grin.

I took my bag which had only shoes, water bottle and sweaty jersey and helped Suhas with his huge backpack. I wonder his back pack weighs as weight as his, so heavy it is!!. I'm waiting for "Vijayawada" board with black letters on yellow board and here it is. I feel so happy to reach place in time. Once we got down, saying thanks to ticket collector, he grins and says " All the best for your game!". *Not bad, they are not as bad and selfish as I thought.*

No sooner our Charminar train passed, we looked at another train on 2nd plat form with board
                    "AP VISHAKA EXPRESS",
 The train which Suhas had to board with his university teammates. The train which he had to board at 17:40, with no worries to pursue his dreams!

we made it!!

We didn't mind our stinky smell. We hugged each other with joy. I jumped with joy and told, "we did it, let's go".

 I ran faster with excitement and Suhas managed to cope up with me, carrying a huge backpack. As soon as we got on to the train. We started calling Suveen, who is on train going for Tennis university games.

As ever, Suveen responded like he is out of the world.

 "Suveen where are you?, we are on the train, which coach are you in?" I talked to him anxiously.

"what?!!!!!!"

"we are on the train and tell me your coach number."

Before he responds , train gave a jerk and   started moving. No more Suhas needs my company, his teammates will take care of him. I got off the train saying bye to Suhas.

I was smiling and walking. Looking at me in shorts with muddy flip flops, one of the cops standing on plat form asked me about my whereabouts.

"My friend is going to Bhubaneswar", with relaxed tone I replied.

"But this train goes to Secunderabad!!!." He exclaimed with sympathetic tone.

✓

Part 2

Return journey,

No sooner, cop told Karthick, He realized that the
engine is heading towards the opposite way his last
train went.

He started panicking, the moment he was told about
wrong train, he spurred like a mad dog and started
shouting," Suhas, Suhas get off the train",

"Suhas! get off the train, pull the chain! you are on the
wrong train", he was worried like hell, as, if Suhas
goes to other place, he'll face problems to come back
or reach Bhubhaneshwar, and to consider importantly
his phone is running out of charge.

Karthick was running till the platform ended and
then with cautious steps, he still ran on gravel, and
yeah call it wonder! or any word in this world, train
has slowed down and halted, he was least bothered
about the reason and it stopped. Without Suhas
pulling the chain, he got down and was devastated.
Suhas was so worried and was in a shock.

Suhas looked at me with morose face saying, "How
now?"

Vexed with series of problems, I moved backward to the enquiry counter asking for trains to Bhubaneswar. Luckily, we have a special train at 3, directly to Bhubaneswar, he has to go alone all the way to Bhubaneswar, I recognize, he can't, but for the universities sake, he needs to! I got ticket to Bhubaneswar and handed it to Suhas.

"This is our last option, nothing can be done now, you've to travel alone".

With so much of hesitation, he took the ticket and started preparing mentally for the journey. We threw our bags down and rested. I was starving and so does Suhas. We brushed teeth and had very early morning breakfast. Suhas started in search of socket to pin his phone for charge. I had a good nap and was woken up with the sharp voice of unknown girl telling me about the arrival of train. We sat in the station waiting for the train and with the latest voice announcement, train is 30 minutes late.

After 30 minutes, another announcement saying 1 hour late, we could do nothing, except, wait for it with exhausted faces.

As soon as the train arrived, we stood rooted to the spot looking at the train. Train is totally jammed with people, sleeper seems like general and general! May god save the people who are in it. Whichever coach you see, people are sleeping on floors, 3 people are sleeping on one berth, with hardly breathing space in the train. There is no place even near toilets. Everything seemed full, jammed. It was jaw dropping for both of us to have the sight.

Suhas voiced his fear, saying that he didn't want to go.

As ever, I started searching for Ticket Collector. Like ants on sugar, people rounded the ticket collector. I manage to go front and ask for a berth till Bhubaneswar. Ticket collector gives me a weird laugh "Go! there is berth beside driver". I stood still, waiting for him to flush his sarcasm aside and give berth. He didn't. With so much of impatience, he left the place and we are in shock. Looking at train which resembles worst than public toilet. I could sense the fear in Suhas and told him not to worry, "we'll make it."

I started running behind ticket collector and requested him for the berth. Starting with request I ended at begging, still the result is failure. With less minutes in our hand I came near Suhas

"For the universities sake, you need to do this, one journey can push you to pursue your dreams".

Suhas didn't get convinced. As the loco pilot revved the engine, I look at the train, Suhas and the annoying ticket collector. I said what I needed to, and he had to decide. Before train gains speed, he step onto the train standing at the edge of train and says bye.

Suhas got on to the train!!!!, he want to achieve his dream. I can't let him face any more problems. Looking at his petrified face, I ask him to give me place to place my foot on train.

While train sped away from station, we both found little place to fit our asses and travelled in the most unpleasant jammed train.

Whatever the situation be, When needed, I'm always present, to help my friend.

With drained out face, I returned to Hyderabad in ac train after dropping Suhas in universities.

Mad &Matured

In love.

In the bridge of relation, she talks, I listen. she shouts, I please. I shout, she pleases. She cries I concern. We laugh. We love. We live.

From high school love to aged love, the form of expression may change, but not the feelings.
In past days, people expressed through letters. Now, they talk through text messengers.
We are 90 kids in between the bridge of 2milleniums, 2 centuries, 3decades.

We feel so happy to be in our world keeping our moments in private, in secret. I'm so happy that we are not lovers spreading our love virtually, socially!. I don't talk to Amu with status on Whatsapp, but through words on real paper. I don't tag Amu in Instagram, but I put our photo in my journal writing about the moment. I don't put a long status on Facebook stating my love to her, but I write a very long mail to her.

Telling her, "I Love you" on face, than on Facebook contents me.

A hug in high school love, is all mattered, so does in old couple love. Romance is what fuels the feelings to express love, to live in love. Like everyone, we had our own style of romance. We romanced through senses, we romanced through silence. We romance through words, we romanced through worldly things.

All we together, craved for space in, is beach, woods, mountains, nature. We love the long walks we take after the practice. We love the loneliness we spend at bus bay. When lovers in the world are busy scoring the bases, we are busy in romancing through fights, frowns.

✓

When it is about, attending parties, smoking and drinking. Amu never restricted me, putting conditions. She always pleaded me to do anything in limits.

I attended my friend's birthday party and was exhorted to drink. Starting with one peg, it continued with, fizz, grog, on the rocks, sling, flame shots and it never ended, until I made a huge mess in the party.

I woke up on my bed with worst hangover ever.

After looking at my phone I realized, I put something on fire, I've talked to Amrutha for 94 fucking minutes, OMG! Without any second thought I called her voicing my fear. Without even saying hello, she orders me to come to home.

With so many questions running on my mind, I start to home after hot shower. I visit her home like dignified boy in formals. Ringing her door bell, I wait outside the door, expecting her father and mom being busy in home. She opened the door and wished me with slap.

She slapped me as soon as she saw me. I became sure about what I have done last night. *Something terrible..* Silently I entered home.

"sorry".

She doesn't make an eye contact with me with infuriated face. She frowns and doesn't talk to me. Before I start apologizing,

With harsh tone," give me word that you're not going to drink or smoke", she ordered.

I sat silently .

"Karthick, why the heck you talked such rubbish, I'm so mad at you for what you did last night", She shouted.

The awkward moment when you know that you made mess, but not what exactly you did. I sat silently without lifting my head.

After her heavy preaching, "You're becoming too dominant", I said.

"Yes I am!!! idiot, I know how to be nectar, and also sometimes chilly!", she told without any mercy.

I stood silently, thinking about what I could have done or said that was so bad.

"Never ask me what you did yesterday!!!! I'm never going to recollect it, the worst conversation between us ever", she said, and continued preaching.

I sit calmly, sadly listening to her words.

"Sorry, I never meant to hurt you, I want to change to be good, to be with you."

"I won't smoke and drink."

I sat on couch, looking down without making an eye contact. She comes near me, ruffles my hair , " Paavi, tell me that you won't drink again" . With her fragrance around me, I look into her eyes and said "no I'll never".

she straddles me, "Idiot, I want you to be good, healthy, safe!!, you've hurt me badly last night, It's okay, you accepted your mistake na, it's okay"

And that's how magic started with frown and a lot of fear.

After spending moments with squeezing hugs, I didn't dare to question about what happened last night . When I'm high on Amu's presence, I don't think I need alternatives. We spent insurmountable time embracing each other.

"Karthickuuuuu, I love you", she said and kissed me holding my hair tight and made me all red with her love bites.

From guilt to love, we started romancing and hit the bases without making home run; saving the best for later.

Night at terrace

After a hot shower, and heavy dinner, I sit down at balcony listening to "Luka chuppi" lullaby. After listening the melodious mellowed song depicted on the occasion of death, wondering how ironic is the lyrics and situation. I stay there sitting calmly, looking at dark bluish sky with black lined clouds, and pristine white moon in midst of bow of blue clouds. With flashing thunders, lightning struck in sky with blaring sounds. The view from the balcony is enticing and thought it'd rain. But no, not a drop of water is falling on this land. With cool breeze, flashing thunders, blaring sounds I'm struck in hostel wishing to meet my girl.

Making vehement wish real , I started to Amu's home without giving a thought to consequences. At 23.09 I am at Amu's house, calling her to have a glance at road. She came into her balcony. Looking at road, She jumped with joy. She wished to meet me and I made her wish real. I am on deserted road fearing who'd come and question me,

"After I text you", she said, "Come to terrace".

Karthick is on rounds rounding her house with his phone staring at it for the message. Waiting for a second, made him sage, the moment when he's out of gaze, he's of same age. He was badly waiting for the message.

My phone vibrates with message, "Come to terrace :D ".

My heart started beating so fast, as, I started towards the gate. I slowly open the gate and my heart almost skipped the beat when it gave loud screeching noise. I felt like I'm working on MI-2 mission. After sneaking inside, I managed to close the gate without a creek.

I look upstairs and head towards the stairs. I climb the steps looking for my girl. As soon as I climb the last step and take a turn, searching for my girl, I see her standing at the end of wall, looking at me. I walk towards her, and moon with most dull marks faded away into the deep bluish sky and nothing could shine except my girl's face with radiance.

It seemed the night has stuck in time warp, when I walked towards her. Her fragrance can make withered lilies to blossom. Her fragrance is poison for my docility . I take her into arms and hugs her, wishing how I missed her so much. We stood there, still, hugging each other for moments, seconds, minutes. After countless minutes of cuddle, she says, "karthickkku, Missed you so much da".

I look at her face and say with chortle, "I know".

She hits me, saying, "Do you also know that I'm
going to punish you for coming late?.".

She slaps me sweetly and place her head on my heart
and says, "How did you know that I was missing you
and wishing to meet you?".

I look at her eyes and said, "Because even I was
missing you and wishing to meet you, so here
I am o my gorgeous lady,"

She laughs and walk away from me, I hold her hand
and take a stroll on terrace.

Walking slowly, while breeze caressing my face,
smooth hands holding me. Listening to soothing
voice of my honey, I lie down stretching my arms on
the floor and my girl joins me resting her head on my
arm and together we gaze at the sky, stars and the
beautiful night. We both love spending the time in
nature without buzz of humans. Once again we are
lost in our talks, starting with the topic of star that is
shining so brightly to the angels lining up for the
construction of bridge from my love's door step till
moon. We started ruling worlds, kingdoms and so
silly were the conversations, one would go mad
witnessing the conversation. Words were the language

of our love in the whale of time spoken through senses, silence, soul.

Amu: I'm there. Your saviour, you need not have worries.

Me: *Laughs* yes saviour.

Amu: I will take care of you.

Me: Ok my mistress! no, no, ok my angel.

Amu: hmmm u r my most precious subject
my mistress is perfect. I am no angel.

Angels are fragile; breakable

Amu: So what are our ministers and courtiers saying?
    how are the state affairs going on?

Me: all our ministers are following same rule,
        "Eat, rave, repeat."

Amu : My kingdom is the whole world
        and the underworld also the
        upper world if it exists.
        All are my subjects,
        My man, take me to the paradise.
        earth. Let's spread the love there

Me: Let me give you piggy back ride till earth, my love.

We are mad, utterly mad, and high on love. We laugh, thinking what are we up to?. We live in our fantasies and rule our kingdom, I'm happy. I'm happy, sleeping here with my girl gazing at stars and having endless talks. While my soul frame the feelings through (the) lines, I tell her gazing at the sky,

Here I come with loving heart
to see your calm face, my sweet heart

Here I come to see my beauty
curling her up in bed

Here I come to see you
covering up mile
and you give me is loving
Hearty smile

Here I come to give you gentle kiss
&cuddle you, baby feel our bliss

Here I come to wish my girl a
Good happy morning!

" Kalai vanakkam anbu[3]", Amrutha with tingle said.

I smile and tell some lines in Kannada and end up with beautiful lyrics from movie,

"Nanu ninnanu preetisithudene " , and then beautiful song lyrics "Ennodu Nee Irunthaal, Uryirodu Naan Iruppen."

"Ennai Naan Yaarendru Sonnaalum Puriyathey" , She joins me singing, "cinema songs venda da".

"Ninna manassininda helu. Mounadallu ninna Preetiyannu arthamaadikollaballe[4]"

Listening to her Kannada lines, With submissive tone I said, "I can understand what you mean, but no, please don't torture with world languages, if you are angry on me... Please."

She gently get on me, bestriding, while I lie down on the floor. I look at those sparkling eyes, and in a trice, everything has been out focused. Teasing me ,

---

[3] Good morning Love

[4] Speak through your heart, I can understand your love through silence

tendering me she comes close, leaning on me. All I can see is, my love's eyes and we spend moments staring at each other without fluttering eye brows. I could feel her fragrance all over me. Her hair fringes fall over her eyes while she nears me slowly and traces my lips with her soft lips and bite my lower lip with fervour and kisses me. I caress her lips before I rage tongue war with her, I take her into me with my legs around her and slide the hands to touch the soft body, softer than her satin pyjamas.

While she trembles with love, passion. I ease her kissing gently and kiss her on forehead, eyes, cheeks, ears and whispered "Nīṅkaḷ eṉ picācāṉavaṉāl[5]." And gently bite her ear which is big turn on for her and cuddled her, lying on the floor, with open sky while stars witness our romance. Moon moves with jealousy looking at our love. She pulls me into her and kiss me on neck like vampire sucking the blood, she leaves a deep reddish mark on my neck and kisses on my heart and leaves a strong lip mark on shirt. "I sign on your shirt and your heart to tell everyone in this world that, you belong with me!"

I stare into her eyes, with accepting thought, "Whatever you say, My devil."

---

[5] You are my devil

Before sun takes its place, I started to hostel, wishing my girl, good happy morning and left the house without letting the gate creak.

"Let this semester go, I'll study from next semester", with these kind of thoughts, last day preparation lasted only for 1st year. Last day preparation got shortened to last hour preparation. Confidence has risen to over confidence. Knowingly wrote hall ticket number, details. Unknowingly wrote answers and filled too many sheets. Whatever it is, passed 2nd year of engineering with 75.3% with no backlogs.

3 Months of holidays. 3 Months of joblessness. Every branch planned Industrial tour a.k.a North India tour. EEE branch planned early and is leaving early.

Send off

Me: Take care.

Amrutha: 79

Me: What?

You told 79 times to take care, common Karthick, I'd be jumping with joy if those were some other words, talk something else.

Me: "I know".

Amrutha: You know everything na, go sleep!!!

Me: venda, venda[6], You told, you missed giving me something besides books and Dvd?

Amrutha: Yeah, nothing important, I'll show you later.

As clock is ticking, we are lost in world of 'us'. Discussions from the fly's bite on the forehead to the specifications of NASA space shuttle for our 9th honeymoon were all talked on phone, I am so

---

[6] In tamil, "NO"

restless after practice, but since these are the last hours before Amu leaves for Delhi. I'm getting strained with late night love. And I still talk while I chew coffy bite to deprive drowziness. Laughing at our own jokes, blushing for sweet scoldings, scolding for silly, sweet mistakes and cherishing each and every moment in the world of "us", we never put the phone down and time is 3.13 am. As me and my phone ran out of charge, I told her, "Take bath and start for the station, and happy journey, take care".

Amrutha : 105!

Me: Love you.

Amrutha: I know.

Amrutha started missing Karthick from the moment she started to the railway station. when Karthick told, " Bye", he could sense her disappointment. He wants to make her smile while she is leaving Hyderabad. He want to see her smile. He want to wish her happy journey for 106th time. He start to station at early morning hitch hiking.

Amrutha gets into the station with weary face looking down, and I look at her expressionless face and smile staring at her.

Her eyes sparkled with my surprise and she was
stunned. She stopped walking front. she removed her
hood and ruffled her hair and gazed at me, blinking
her eyes frequently surmising the present.
 My girl is looking so beautiful even without proper
sleep, she is stunning, like surreal art piece in her blue
hoodie and black jeans, wearing a backpack, a true
expeditioner, polyglot, knows 5 languages but not
Telugu,

*Beauty is not what delineates you, but defines your
thought.*

Yes, my baby is beautiful in her soul and her thought.
My smiley face changed into surprised face in trice.
Even I have my piece of surprise, here comes her clan
Surprising me.

Malayalam mother, Tamilian father, Telugu son in
law, Karnataka daughter.

I am so interested to mail my story as, "4 states" to
Chetan Bhagat.

I am introduced as, "good friend" to her mother,
father, and a couple of cousins. They greeted me with
a smile. And to be eased, with future in laws, I start
conversation blabbering about weather, water, warm
clothes and what not!. I spoke to her parents long

71

enough for them to let me talk freely with their daughter.

Amrutha with pink face, whispered "Love you".

I was forbidden to do anything except give a laugh in front of their parents and cousins who girded me. I stood calmly, looking into her eyes in the midst buzz of the railway station, comprising my future in laws, taut ticket collector, toiling labour, ginger fragrant tea maker and sirening train with stars fading away into the sky, moon waiting for the sun to take its shift.

Breaking the silence between us, She said, " thanks."

I sang through the silence, saying "I LOVE YOU".

She smiled and said through silence, "I KNOW".

We had our duet, in the midst of dangling stars, smoked up clouds, whispering, how we take the treat of this meet into our cherished album of memories.

As the train started moving, her mother hurried me to get on to the train, I chuckled, and said, " I came to give send off to friends". With a shocked face, surprised face, she says something in Malayalam, which are not in my Malayalam dictionary. But I'm sure her expressions seemed to pity me, but not getting pissed off. By reading her expressions I could translate her saying, " Oh my poor boy, you came all the way to give send off to your friends, go safe,". How lucky I am!, to have such a sweet mother in law, easy person to count on.

I thank god and pray, "Heavenly father, bless me with a brain full of south Indian languages, Kannada to flatter my girl, Tamil to seek permission from her father, Malayalam to butter her mom to accept the proposal. I know it is a bit difficult for you to bless me with so much of brain power to speak all these languages, simply bless their family with love to accept me and I'll manage with English in the family.

1 THE END

With legs crossed, Karthick sat on the floor at a
corridor staring at the sky in shock.

Gloominess suppressed the glow. Silence settled,
muting the strings of harmony in the home.
Euphonious voice which reverberated, has gone
silent, making everyone silent in shock. The home
is filled with the incense sticks' fragrance, leaving a
glowing ember, smouldering. And flowers floored
the centre of the hall calming the intense emotions
of pain. Relatives are raging against god for what he
did.

While Amrutha's mom pleased Amrutha to open
her eyes, her father with no moral support, stood in
support of pillar weeping for her. In midst of home,
In presence of loving people, Amrutha with
gleaming eyes, stills in photo with garland around it
and lamp infront of it. Death of the only daughter
had not only shocked, also desolated everyone.

Cloudburst wreaked havoc in families of students.
Media outraged for a day and two   on   natural
calamity. Everyone gathered at amrutha's home,

mourning for bereavement. People gathered in groups listening to friends, while they describes the incident. "Sun at its dusk, setting down at 5.40 pm. Reclining the seat back we were looking outside, nature. It was a giant curve of a river stretch by side, paved for water flow. Stretch of rocks fenced with mountains and a road on one side. All of us looked at the stones in the middle of the stretch with back ground of mountains, green trees with no sillohouette.

Pebbles were wet with stream of water, very low stream that it couldn't wet whole feet till ankle if stood there. Everyone got down looking at beautiful stretch of rocks and got onto rocks taking selfies, photos in groups. Everyone, happily with embrace of nature, enjoyed the moment, with friends, with love. There were 4 rocks in ascending and more people occupied 4th rock located at center of the stretch. Some of the people went to temple praying. 60 of us occupied all the rocks , enjoying and enticing to get into natures warmths. Cooling the climate, everyone were caressed by a cool breeze, then drizzle, then rain, and then flood.

In no time, rain rushed heavily, drenching us in a trice. Simultaneously, river in spate and we were shocked, panicked to get out of it. The rocks were covered half in fraction of seconds & while everyone held each other in dire moments, the strong current swept some of my friends, Amrutha was on 3rd rock and helped our friends to move quickly to the land and before she could run out of danger, she was swept away with strong stream of water leaving us."

Karthick was still as statue, looking deeply at her bruised face, without shredding any tear. Nectar of his life made his mind numb. Not with any thought. Not with any emotion. He stared at her, covered in white cloth making everyone cry. His senses could not sense about his love's death. He was in shock looking at her. Being still, being numb.

While Amrutha's mother pleases her to open eyes, She was put into a coffin to sleep forever in midst of land. I join their family, carrying her for the one last time. Loved a long walk with her, and now is the final walk with her, carrying her on me for the last, ever time.

She hopped on me, rounding my neck with her hands. I carried her, walking on a long road and she gave me goosebumps exhaling her breath and whispered ," Will you carry me Life long?" with giggle.

Now I want to say, "YES".

Mourning for her, didn't calm the exacerbated pain.

Church Father requested everyone to share some words about her. I stood beside the coffin, trembling to speak and see my love. In stammered voice,

"Amrutha, Amm...ru..tha always smiles and make others smile in life, She is like the serene sky being calm and spreading love, goodness. Sweetest woman on the earth. Last time I took her on me, for a piggy back ride, and now I carry her in coffin........"

Karthick outbursts with tears, placing a hand on her head. With vehement emotion, he cried and still couldn't let out all the pain crying for days and days and days.

REMINISCES

Wearing the light blue shirt, Karthick visited her
home with the roses in hand and the letters in
covers. Looking at Amrutha, she happily smiled
through her eyes, making his day special. She
looked charming as ever with her hair loose and
curls bit curled at the end, gleaming eyes, hovered
to shower the love and scoldings, for wearing a dull
blue shirt. He looked at her lip marks on shirt and
placed his fingers on it, where her lips conquered
his heart, with her sign leaving marks on shirt.

With Karthick's presence,
Past became her part, ignoring it.
The future became forever far to look for, and
present, so pleasant with the reason of his presence.

Karthick sat down looking at her and fell in her
trance.

Karthick looked at her, walking on an empty road,
escorted with green trees on either side and flowers
to embellish the mother nature. He saw her face
with glow, where NASA scientists cannot measure
it. With Sun taking leave, accepting the defeat for

incapability of outshining her in his life. While birds
tweets' tuning up the world, he found the treasure,
his love, and stared at her, struck to express what
he means and she looked so cute, melting him to
cuddle her with love. He took her into him, placing
his hand around her slim waist and walk. With
several months training, she managed to learn
broken Telugu and said " po da", which she learnt
on first day. He took her into his world, embracing
her with love and walk. While she rests her face on
his shoulder, eyeing at him for the way he is. She
looked with immense happiness by looking at
pleasing smile on his face.

Karthick looked at, her staring at him, and it's
inevitable to rise from, falling for her, (from abyss
a.k.a love) again and again. Before he opens his
mouth to say the sweet words, she placed her hand
to stop his words and said, *" Do not live in me, leaving
me, Let me live in you, leaving you."*

Karthick shred tears wetting the lip marks
whenever he visits this place. She looked at him
with a calm face, contagious smile. He places his
hand on his heart, letting his love, know that she is
still in his life and kissed her through air staying a
few feet away from her photo. She is lying

underneath grains of salt and land. she is in him,
leaving him from this world,

Karthick took the roses and letters and leave her
tomb, new home, praying for uncle and aunt to give
peace in their life.

Even after a month, Memories and all the moments
related to her, haunted him. He felt, he should meet
her parents to give support and ask support.

TALK WITH TAMILIAN DAD

Entering home, I looked at blue colored walls,
embellished with frames of photos of my love and
her family's. I gazed at a photo of her, snapped by
me while she was busy in writing a fair copy of my
write up on, "World at its worst scenario". Here I
am looking at her, with my world in the worst
scenario without her, and her smile.

She has a serene face blessed with charm in that
photo, photogenic face!. I was welcomed by her
parents and I sat on the couch in front of aunt &
uncle with a box full of photos, fragranced papers

with penned poems, letters, and the lip marked dull
blue shirt.

I sat in front of them to tell,

" Nothing is there to recall, as everything is still in
me, hurting me, killing me.

I take this minute, with shame, to tell about our
love, our relation. We were taking care of each
other and had wonderful relation and she is no
more with me.

To tell about our love, she started living in me,
leaving this world.

We are in love & wanted to convey it to you, after
we come to a position to commit to each other, to
support each other mentally, economically. I'm not
here to put pull stop to this love and start pursuing
love with others. I'm in love with your daughter,
she has left me so much of love, that I don't regret
stating I'm alone without love.

I don't dare to put myself in your position and
think. With a year of love, and loads of moments,
I'm in shock to believe about her dismissal. And I

don't dare to think about you people, who gave everything to let her grow, shine in this world. With your love and caring, she has become the finest being in this world.

Uncle, aunt! She is in heaven hearing us, she doesn't like us being moody, sad. She loves the smile on both of your faces, there is nothing in this world that she'll not try, to make both of you have peaceful, happy life.

Now in this point of life, I need to heal myself from this hurricane of her pass away, I need to explore myself and my dreams and live, pursuing it. I need time, I need your support with your forgiveness for fobbing you by hiding our relation. Please forgive me."

But no, not a word uttered and we sat in silence for countless minutes.

Looking at me with box of all memories, Amrutha's father broke the silence, "we are glad to know how you obliged to our love and care." Her father with stuttering voice, "In a span of an evening, my world has turned dark with the dismissal of my daughter, the only endeared pampered child",

Taking time and surmounting silence, he said, "she had this letter written for you in her bag, take it. Keep it with you, somethings are not meant to hide, in fear of recalling the worst past, but those are meant to keep it with us, to avoid going astray and to seek support during sadness."

Dear karthickuuuuuuuu

A call for snap
Poke during a nap
I only find "YOU"
A call for stroll in college
Straddle on terrace
It is you, only you

My sweet pie, though not as good as you, I write something for you with my heart, with love. It had been happy hours of my life since the moment I met you. If I start a series of how I met your father, I make sure I'll end within 4 series,

our 4 nights <3 . You were
there with me through thick
and thin, pampering me like
my father, guiding me like my
mother. I'm in awe to have a
boy friend like you, who put up
with me all the time. I'm your
pesterer, supporter. I cherish all
the moments you made for me.
The reason I smile is you, the
reason I cry is you, you are
the reason for this eternal
emotion of being valued,
respected, taken, loved, cared,
carried. The way you respect
my mom and dad, for being my
parents, is out of what I can
explain. Hope these days
without you will make me cry
for all the times I have
annoyed you through.(hard
times,)You were always there

taking care of me like you are looking after a toddler.

Thickuuu I miss you alot, don't stay awake at nights, take care of your health. Finish all these books before I return, to reach into you, cuddling you. I leave with so much of sadness, and also smile, to not let you down during my absence. Take care. And hope you make me fall in love with your words and poems, again and again and until this earth stops revolving. Here I gift you, your favorite movie DVD, Dead poets society, Keep writing and also keep missing me. With love.

AMU

xxxx

Tears rolled, while Karthick read the letter taking it into his hands, she has written many letters, but not anything before she left. She never left him for long times, but now suddenly she left him supposedly forever. He sat at his table looking at the letter, and craving for her presence. With a pen in his hand, he inked the words from his heart craving for her presence, smile.

1, 2, 3, 4
Am always at your door
2, 3, 4, 4
Wanna make you fly high from floor
3, 4, 4, 4
Please stand with me on the shore
4, 4, 4, 4
Baby, I'm craving to see you with love
and make your face glow.

***

Never know, if I can love what I have
Want to know, what more do I have?

Does this nature know,
I'm not me who I was last day

Singing with cry of love
Moaning with miss of mirth

I'm not me, who I was
Last second, last minute

As every breath I take,
is not complete with miss of my love.

I pack all my stuff, starting to the place, where Amu stood at last, taking her last breath. I want to visit the place, where she lost her life. I wants to see how hard it was for her, to stay in those worst conditions. I took leave for Delhi, to reach the place with straying thoughts, with no one next to me to listen my nightmares.

ABHINAY RENNY

Living with endless hope
Sliding away with force

Blessed is the water when it heals
cursed is the water when it kills

Baffling with, no human mind

Singer has gone mute in frost
But her music still reverberates

Where can I find the warmth wish
Whenever I cross our lord's pitch

Water may take away the breathe
but not the unblemished soul

Leaving the flesh, stricken
living in the hearts of heaven

24/7 from heaven
Wishing me to cherish the life

Sailing the ship of my life

Moving forward a mile
recalling her smile.

Not once
but forever!!

As the bus took a steep curve and reach a broad
road, having a small bypass way to the small sand
dunes ,to the river. Enough place to halt the trucks,
and so much of a place to stay there, and look at
the scenery. Karthick got down at a place called,
Sanli where Saveri river flows by, in midst of two
mountains.

Karthick slowly got down, walking through the
sand into the dried up vast stretch. He looked at
small pebbles which made him so huge. And he
looked at the giant rock making him tiny before it.
There were series of rocks scattered all over the
stretch, There were also 4 rocks placed till the
centre of the stretch from sand. He moved to the
centre of the stretch, on the 3rd rock. He stood up
on the rock, looking at the huge mountains on
either side of the river with trees on it. A steep
curve at the end of sight from where water flowed
in sudden. And on the other side, a long stretch
placed with huge rocks. He saw very less people
scattered in the mountains cutting trees.

Karthick looked up at sun, covered with clouds
and collapsed on the rock, with tears in his eyes

rolling. He sat on the rock and gazed at the stretch,

Amu after the nap, looked at the mountains while
the bus took a steep curve getting down to reach
Delhi. Looking at two mountains nearby, and a
river stretch in between, with low stream of water,
made a beautiful scenery urging to capture the
moments. When everyone got down, she slowly got
down and opened her hands full, whirling to look
at the heaven, with mix of mountains with trees,
water with rocks, and people, scattered being busy
in their lives.

No sooner Amu got down into water, she jumped.
Water is frigging cold, she couldn't hold her foot
for more than 2 minutes, she felt so cold and got
onto the rock clicking selfies, group pictures with
everyone.

As the sun sets down, the view from the rock, to
look at the sun captured between two mountains
and a long stretch, with the cool breeze caressing
everyone. It was beautiful.

Drizzle drastically changed the moods of people
from happiness to ecstasy. Drizzle didn't drench
them. Everyone had smiles on their face looking at

the sky. Amu whirled on the rock enjoying the drizzle. In a trice, light blue sky turned into gravel grey sky, with no sun to give the silver lining. Cool breeze turned into whirled wind, quivering leaves with water droplets flew away. People feeling fresh with petrichor were wished with pitter patters on the rock. Rhythmic sounds turned into whirring voice. The cloudbursts created havoc. Rain rushed drenching everyone.

With thought to return, people started running. Before making the thought real, a gush of water flowed with force washing away the pebbles and small rocks. With so much force, the water took a steep curve turbulating the flow, increasing the force and hit the rocks, also the people who were on it. With bewildered faces, everyone panicked looking at water, flowing heavily with force. Amrutha helped Ashritha to move to the other rock, and in the nick of time, her imagination of beautiful sunset passed away.

Nothing, she could see except, water rushing, taking away the life of her friends.

She stood in shock, looking at her friend flowing into the river and then was her chance, taken away

with water, hitting the rocks and flowing in 2
degree Celsius cold water. Water not only caressed
her, but also crushed her. No one was tolerated
with a terrific roar of nature. Calm nature turned
terrific, erratically taking the lives. Water with heavy
force, dangled the lives of many, taking away from
this world. Within minutes, with cold temperature
and bruised face and head, she took a last breath in
shock and rest the body in the body of water.

Karthick looked at her, Swaying in the water with
debris of woods, gasping for the air. Toiling
through water and seeking for help, none could
look at her. Drowned in water and head hitting the
huge rocks, and receiving shocks with hits on rocks
and cold water freezing the blood in the body.

Karthick took out the letter and read it loud, with
cry of love and pain.

After reaching down from the rock, I looked at soft
pebbles and wondered how the nature is so calm at
times and also terrific at times, It is mother nature
which flows, shines, crumbles, breaks, cracks, and
yet, live for millions of years. But living beings on
the board of mother nature, give the life and also
give away the life.

I take a leave from the place where my love, Amu took her last breathe and sit at railway station with plethora of thoughts running in my mind. I look at India map looking at blue area, wondering what if once water, which fills earth 3/4th, decides to erupt on and vanish the small part, land. 7 billion lives would perish in a moment of earth's rotation. And then later, still sun shines, water flows, snow falls. Pandemonium nature.

Thinking about nature, I recall how myself and Amu love nature and beaches. We've always fantasized our engagement in houseboat in Kerala backwaters, marriage at beach shore, and first night in an island. I decide to go for beach, to spend the nights with my love, beach and Amrutha.

❖

Goa times

After 38 hours of travel, I reached Goa and
checked into hotel near Kerim beach.

Without wasting any second, I doze off falling into
bed with so much of stress mentally, physically.
After 14 hours of sleep, I feel bit okay after severely
stressed out horrible journey from Delhi to Goa.

Being famished, I took a bath and rushed to food
joint. I managed with Konkani language which I
learnt in starting of my 2nd year, After the brunch,
I stroll, heading to the beach and the moment I
stepped onto the sand watching sky teeming to
water. I am scared. Never had been this moment!!! I
am scared to look at the water, I am scared to look
at the curbing waves, making thundering sounds in
my ears, I close my eyes taking time for myself,
breathing slowly. Nothing works and I am hell
scared with each and every step I put towards
water. Sudden morbid fear of water took all over
me, creating havoc in mind.

I took all my energy, strength supporting myself to
act calm and ignore Amu's utter shrill of cry. I see

Amu struggling to hold on to the rock, before she got into a spate of river, I see Amu panicking with helplessness, I see her drowning in chilled water where she couldn't even held her foot for 2 minutes. I see her legs twitching with constricted hands. I see her crying for the help while her knee gets broken with hit of rock. I see Amu gasping for the air, moving hands uncontrollably . I close my eyes and hold my head to flush the thoughts, clearing the horror in my mind. I'm frazzled, I return to room without giving another glance at the beach, water, and the shore.

I returned to the room with frazzled mind and body. Water exacerbated the pain, it reminded the struggle of my love. This is the first time I was treated badly by the beach, Avalanche of emotions deprived my sleep. I look up, staring at the sky from balcony, wondering what this world still has for me.

Goa is great for alcohol lovers, but a bit difficult for teetotalers obtaining good healthy food. Finishing brunch, I didn't dare to go for beach under the hot sun. I took nap in my room and slowly got out after the sun got out of Goa's sight.

With determined mind, I brought up all the energy
I had, and after a series of self suppositions, "Amu
takes me to beach with love,! Amu takes me to
beach with love!, " saying so many times within
myself. I braced myself for the war where my mind
is getting crushed, with thoughts of horror and
struggle.

I took out the portrait of Amu from bag and
looked at her, she smiles supporting me saying,
"*embrace me with love*". I stared at the photo holding it
in my hand, I wipe my tears off the portrait. And
looking at her eyes. I get so much of support from
her eyes, which says, *"Even if the world ends, I wish to
end my life with you,"*. I swiped the tears on porttrait,
saying to myself, I'd not let myself struggle now,
with thoughts of struggle of Amu.

Amu can't look at me while I'm in this trauma.
How can I forget that she has really undergone
through that trauma. My mind swayed with
thoughts, crippling me on bed. I spent nights
staying in room, being idle, being stock still, not
high with weed, but low with shock. After spending
so many days in the same room, I stood up and said
to myself, "Water may take away the breathe, but

not unblemished soul, Girl take me to the water!
My Amu is still with me.
"Amu lives with me, lives in me, I shall not let
myself and also her with these thoughts."
I slowly headed to beach, where Goa is lit with
luminous lights. Moon replaced the sun, I head to
beach and stepped onto the sand while air caressed
me. With frames of Amu's struggle flaring up. With
fear, with horror, I slowly started moving onto the
sand and finally look at waves, roaring to curb the
land, tides reaching land by tearing the silence. All
except waves, is what I'm unknowingly ignoring.

It's not as small as moon to shell it's light with
hand, It is not as small as a star to stop with finger
from sight, it is blue water, spread all over the land,
bellowing at me reminding me, the struggle my love
faced.

I stood, staring at those venturesome fishermen
going into the water to get fish, earning livelihood
for their family. The water may have taken away
their loved one's lives, but still, they go into it
embracing it, feeling it, and living on it.

Though I closed my eyes, the water roars with its
waves and tides trembles me with frames of my

love's struggle. Taking all the mental trauma, I
removed my shoes and sat in the place where
waves are at sight,

I don't want to go, touch the water. I sat on the
sand looking at the beach, no one could grab my
attention except the water. I sat for hours staring at
beach with so many thoughts about Amu.

I'd always tell her about beach bride. I used to tell
her, how I wish to marry on a beach at the crack
of the dawn.

 "While beach blooms with the sun, subtle sun rays
falls on water giving mix of blue shades. At blue
water on one side, green trees on other side. White
silicon sand sailing from centre less water to land
forming berms and cusps. A long red carpet,
spread for bride to walk with her father. A pristine
white tent, with no cover on 4 sides for a church
father, to conduct the wedding.

 Limited chairs, covered with light blue satin cloth.
I stand on the sand while I fly in cloud nine. I wait
for the beautiful bride in a black tuxedo .

"If you wish to marry at beach, I want to wear
beach bride dress" , she'd always tease me telling.

"what is a beach bride dress?"

" Beach bride dress is bikini", she'd say with giggle.

With so many memories, moments I stared at the
beach sitting on sand, lonely at 1 am realizing, I'm
left alone with water in this 7billion populated
world.

Tears rolled in the eyes,

I am lost in thoughts and suddenly, I shouted with
a cry,

Alone! I am alone!

I am Loner!!!!!

I sing the lines with a cry,

"I am a loner,
chosen by my love to choose it

not this time, I love it.

ABHINAY RENNY

I am shut in this world
crying in my world."

No creature on earth could have imagined Karthick
sitting on the beach, alone without anyone at night.
Karthick looks at the water which curbed his love,
he is scared that he'll be driven to get near his love
by getting near the water. He is scared that he will
be hypnotized by the water waves, nearing him with
the rhythm of ricketiness. He looks at darkness,
from which water is rising, welcoming to take him
near his love, Amrutha.

Looking at the water in the light of dull moon and
stars, he stood staring at it, looking at those waves
rushing forward to welcome him and backing
waves to take him back to his girl. In the trance
state of mind, darkness took all over him
magnetizing him towards it. He starts stepping
towards it with oblivious state of mind. His feet,
rushed towards the darkness and eyes are set, to
abyss behind the water, he moves forward,
languidly looking at dark way paved in front of him.
He moves into water touching the waves which are
welcoming him to death, darkness, meet of
enamour, Amrutha.

He wades into water in trance and as soon as he got
pushed away with a strong wave of water, he fell
into the water, which seemed like cyclone curbing
inside, he twitched his hands, legs, gasping badly,
His mind busted with baffle running in his mind.
He twitches his hands to get out of the water, to get
out of the hard knocks. The Body quivers with
coldness, shock making his body numb. With
crippled mind, exhausted body, he tried and tried
and tried and gave up to give his life to the water,
which took his love and now him. Before he gets
washed away in waves selflessly, in a trice,
fisherman who are on their night sail into the sea,
took him, rescued him.

May be, his parents far away from him wanted him
to stay alive. May be Amu wanted him to stay in
this world. May be his friends wanted him to look
at him alive, May be the world wanted him to live,
and spread love.

He was taken back to fisherman's wharf and they
looked after him. Fisher men saw him shivering in
cold and shock. They helped him with rugs and
after he came to senses. He request them to take
him to his hotel, they dropped him and left him in

his room.

With exploded mind, He returned to his room and fell on bed with so many hallucinations; his struggle in the water , running out of water , crying inside the water.

Last night has set him to the reset.

After 13 hours of sleep, He woke up at evening and thinks,

I am all lethargic to do any activity, I felt, me drowning in water, giving up the life. It is all my nightmare at night. It seemed nothing happened at night except, me crying on the beach. Drinking pulpy orange, slowly I go to visit the beach. I stay all night till it becomes deserted and then return to the hotel. This became my routine for days and days and days. I continued going to beach at nights and stay till it's deserted and then leave the place.

One evening before I start to beach, I look at my girl's face and sit at the table and write.

"Learning to be lonely
With you around me

**I'm alone
and you never left me**

**departing not,
loving me
Warts and all.**

With perplexing mind, with thoughts stating, "I'm alone", "Amu is in me, she is with me". I am struggling, holding back my tears.

I know, my girl won't let me groan if she is next to me. My girl is next to me and wiping away my tears.

She always makes me smile with her presence. She wishes to look at me smiling all the time.

My girl kicks me for being moody. She would kick my ass out of this room for this behaviour.

Amrutha!!!!! Sweet like nectar, divine drink to stay immortal, I brood thinking, "my girl couldn't stand up for the name at least". She is Amrutha! My love. She stood up in my life wishing me to spread the love eternally. God!! I came out of the room with the suffocation of air, thoughts.

ABHINAY RENNY

I headed to beach, and with strong belief that beach
will brush away my broodiness, as, my baby ordered
the beach to do so.

I sat on the sand and looped my last thought till I
was tranquilized with the treat of beach. I slowly
started looking at water, which is treating
venturesome fishermen, vaga bonds, couples,
children, loners, veterans and vert equally.

It is water's trait to be serene at times, and terrific
at times. Million years ago water was there, and
flown out of rivers flooding to land. Volcanoes
erupted and burnt the ground. Land cracked and
moved the mountains. Storms sweep, Volcanoes
erupt, land cracks, air swirls, sky thunders.
Dinosaurs lived, ants also lived. Its nature evolving
with its elements. Its nature which evolves with the
same elements in future. In the evolution of nature,
it's humans who born and dies. who comes and
leaves. Its creatures, in this world that needs the
nature.

Nature evolves, Only nature evolves, Once seas are
now deserts, Once forests are now fossil fuels. It's
nature.

With a series of thoughts on the beach and it,
brushing away the brood, I etch on my mind,

Beach breaching the sad shackle

Toddling through tides
Wishing through waves

It's the beach breaking the baffle
It's the beach fleeing over the sand

Roar is the sea's silence
Tranquilizing the nature
energizing the creature

It's the beach, blooming with sun

Bottles rounding the corner
Beach bellowing the anger

Good morning!
Goa is going to sleep.

While I'm thinking about the mysteries of nature, Sun said hi through its beaming rays. I stand up looking at the crack of dawn.

With unagitated mind, I go for room to sleep. Wishing Goa good morning, as, everyone here sleeps at morning and wake up at night, some people being sober, some people surrendering to beer, everyone lives at night. I'm still teetotaler surrounded with beer brawlers bawling, burrowing the bottles in the sand.

With 24 days of stay in Goa, I finally understood the mother nature nurturing the earth in it's own way. Goa became my rehabilitation place. It has been the darkest place during my early times, but now it has treated me, consoled me, cajoled me to get into normal life.

✓

1 THE START

Back to College.

After looking at my room, spiders had special feast making cobwebs in the room. I started wiping the dust off books, photos and clothes. After cleaning my room for hours, I rest myself lying on the bed and look at shelves, covered with sticky notes, photos, novels, diaries, dead poets society DVD and my priceless possessions given by my love; Spirit of music book by A.R.Rahman , a hand made poster. Guitar drawn on the black chart with all the talented artist names in it, starting from the fret board till the end of the guitar, and quote of A.R.Rahman by side,

"I had choice between hate and love, I chose love and here I am"

-A.R.R

I have chosen love and it took me here, and I still choose the same love. Let's see where it takes me.

After a very long break, I visited the college with dread of dear, allaying friends. Everything had changed in college, loss of 34 people had brought the gloominess in college.

With more than a month of extra holidays, everyone took time and rest, to get out of the trauma, but this loss is not something which can be forgotten in a day, month, year. It takes time. I visit my classroom and was into the mob, my friends didn't make me feel awkward, mentioning anything related to her and understood me. They supported me being silent at times. I couldn't sit in class controlling my emotions. Under tree shade, I sit on bench listening to "Jaage hain". It took me to the orchestra room, with full of string section, violins, cellos, conductor, and beautiful music notes of GURU. I sat reminiscing the Roja tunes and started attending classes regularly, atleast for the attendance sake.

Even though If one can't see me in classes, place where everyday one could find me for sure is , the basketball court. The only place I cry is court, I go to court after a month of vacation. Everyone in the team understood me, though I smothered myself, they let me turn every tear drop of cry into sweat wetting the court.

All the negative energy residing in me, turned out into productivity on the court.

My captain cared about me, stood for me when I was crippled in the game and life, the bond I share with my basketball team is very unusual, emotional. The reason I'm standing here, in college with discipline, teamwork, sincerity, is just because of my basketball team. It has shaped my personality to endure in life, during hard times. I spent nights on court exhausting myself to rejuvenate each and every morning, to start a new day and be the beginner of every day.

Writing has been cathartic for me all the time, I emotionally purge from everything and shred the words with heart. I've never stopped writing diary. Sitting in a lonely room, with tranquill state after practice, I ink the feelings...

Walking with joy
In unconscious confusion

Call it distraction
Living in a world
of CARD MANSION

Sailing over sea of people
Not to get drowned
Not to get drenched

ABHINAY RENNY

Circled in a world
Where she was only the world

Seeing the real world
With the pain, peril

Plenty of reasons to strive
Memories dragging to stay in hive

Staying high, to hide my low

Blessed is my life to have my love.
I walk with people along their flow

with blessings of my girl, family and world.
Putting life in proper stow!

With the cycle of practice, college, exams, I'm totally attached to work and I don't have a jobless time to let gloomy thoughts jostle into my mind. With the arrival of technical and cultural fests. To my badness and goodness, I have finally got leisure time everyday, with exhausted mind. I'm always occupied and somehow dragged the cart of life. Now, at this moment, everyone started being busy with fests work in college. Looking at fests, I don't want to get into it, controlling others and being controlled. I'm not scared or incapable to work in worst conditions, I don't want to disturb myself with all negative energy which prevail while working with team of 100 men, I don't think I'm yet ready to deal with that.

Life is taking me where it never took me till now. With so much of time, spent near my table, I'm being cathartic, penning all my feelings, thoughts. I'm reading the same books, countless times to pass the time. Even if I'm getting leisure time of an hour or 2 , I'm either with books, diary, or guitar. I've stopped being on social networking site, since I find everything, blown up in it. As soon as exams are on time, last day preparation has been pushed to last hour preparation. I started cramming before the last minute I enter examination hall. I hate last minute preparation, but to prevail in the port of salient semester ships, I need to work on which I don't like.

Colours triggered me, I started reading about colours and with very keen interest, started learning about street art, graffiti, calligraphy, anamorphic art. Everything seemed interesting, I started searching about all these and wanted to try something, I'm noob who (doesn't even) can't draw even a small diagram, I can play in Auto cad, but not on paper, I manage records and diagrams with friends who gets flattered with my futz. So, I never had problem with drawing figures in my engineering, on paper. As time sailed, I really got into this art and spent each and every spare minute on this art, learning how to perform. I need canvas to perform these kind of arts. Canvas and the currency!. Where can I find the canvas and currency! With all brain storming thoughts, I took the initial step seeking college. During my brainstorming session with myself, I questioned myself, "why will the college provide canvas and currency, what can it expect from me in return, why should it let the amateur".

I found answers to the questions and started digitalizing the answers! I started working on 3 point perspective drawing which gives 3d illusion, one style of anamorphic art. We are taught only 2 point perspective drawing in our engineering drawing, I am applying the basics what I've learnt. I started working on my, "college building drawing" so that, they'll get something to show off, in public during fest time. Before I go infront of fest convener, I got suggestions from seniors who are out of this fest fuss. With all blue prints, cad sheets, I go near fest convener, putting my proposal infront of him. I gave him presentation on the art and convinced him how everyone would post their selfies with this art with #festname and make it viral on the web. After the presentation, I gently walked out of the room with a smile on my face and permission letter in my hand.

Happy Birthday!

I travelled very far, leaving my city, reaching a serene place. I stand on the land, looking at the boat anchored to the wood, water rippling with glint formed by a beam of rays falling on it, the mountains behind the water with dense dark green trees. The Sun stands above the mountains, giving the light to this world. I row the boat through water and reach the mountains. I get into the woods and sit under the shade of the tree to celebrate my girl's birthday here. In midst of trees, water, mountains.

I read out my wishes, I wrote for her on this 20th birthday.

ABHINAY RENNY

Arrives a new day to live
no more a teen to rue

Mellowed is the girl now
moving with mirth

Recreating her own world
by her choice through word

Uttering the happiness
living on the emerging earth

Tousled is her hair
enchanting is her smile

Hailing her all the way
honouring her with tiara

Arrives a new day to live
no more a teen to rue

Happy birthday AMRUTHA!

Tears obscured my vision, obstructing to read.
Wishing my girl, 20th birthday. She is 20 now!!!. She is
no more a teen to rue with adolescence. She is no
more on this earth, making me rue with reminiscence.

She is mellowing girl with merry face, recreating her
world with her choices, loving people, ignoring the
hatred, jealousy,(she always believed in being good to
get good). She knows the importance of happiness,
as, she also know the agony undergone during
sadness. She is Amrutha, ruffling her tousled hair
always with smile. I sit here on this day, celebrating
her birthday gifting her, the most priceless thing for
her, my words, my soul.

Here it is, My words are for you, wish you happy
birthday Amu.

IN the mess.

One fine day, I'm in the mess of the thought process, with various hurdles in front of me.

Completed my 3rd year. When everyone is groaning with GRE,GATE,CAT preparation, I took back, thinking if I can give a try, but being catastrophic, instead of preparing for either examinations blindly , I put my time thinking of what I really want to become.

I had the same question in my mind on my 1st day of my engineering and, still I didn't find the answer, Do I really bother to know the answer?

No, Not until I see the end!!!

Do I think about myself only when I'm idle? Had I ever bared my heart to myself?

 Did I really learned anything in this 3 years of engineering?

Yes!

 Besides learning how to manage without really learning the subject, I learnt to get aggregate percentage of 75 in every semester. Besides learning the objectives of an engineer, I also learnt the loop holes to become a certified engineer.

To say, I learnt many things on the court rather than in mid of four walls of the class. Irrespective of being busy, we the basketball team always attended for practice and always been like family. When I was about to give up my strength, my 1st sailor of the ship, Teja bhai comes with line,

"Things that won't kill you, makes you stronger". Lines are gazillion in this world lacking the soul. But every word spoken by him was rhetoric, rejuvenating, relishing.

What I really want to become?. Do I need to bother or leave the future to the destiny?.

I look at the note on my wall, written,

"The beginning of wisdom is the definition of terms"
-Socrates

Hell with the wisdom, I better think about wisdom, when I'm all with wrinkles. What I really want? Do defining what is what, can give me the answer?

What is passion? What is my passion? Do I have one?

What I think, I'm passionate about, is what I'm really
passionate about? Socrates story defines passion,
every successful person defines passion, but I'm still
unable to find what it is really!!

Do Amrutha know, what I'm passionate about?
Does my team know, what I'm passionate about?

Do I really have one?

What I really love doing ?

I love, living in the moment

 I love to think, I love to express.

I love to write.

I love to live in the moment and express it through
words.

Even Amrutha loved the words of me, She saw my
interest towards poetry, writing.

Can I take my passion as a profession?

"When one's passion becomes the profession,
and then that in turn becomes your obsession,
you are obviously blessed beyond belief."

-A.R.R

I look at the quote on my wall and I'm hit with the
answer I'm searching for.

I have all these quotes since my 1st year, yet, I never
found answer to a question from quote.

Do I ever had questions for myself?

I don't think so.

Words. Wonder how this words influence, Everyone
talks, but only quotes are taken from great
 people, it's not that they say great lines, but they say
through the soul. Words are souls which
transforms people lives. Like music, like painting, like
every art, words are what, which runs the world.
Words are the form of pensive thoughts penetrating
to one's mind when they take it with soul. When one
can find god in the gravel, I can look at lord in the
lines.

ABHINAY RENNY

In every line I speak through my soul, there is God, there is power, there is a force which can thrive the world.

I sit in my room with voices cornering me, shouting at me, " Just do what you love with love, Game is not rocket science". Soothing me, "Karthick, you does magic with your words and I love them". Inspiring me , "Jacob!!, Everyone wants! But question is how badly you want?."

Everyone talked to me, supporting me, but wish, I talk to myself.

How badly do you want?

With baffling thoughts for days, weeks. Decided to do what I love. Realizing, contentment is in us not in the world fuss. I wrote letter to myself to support me, to console me, to embolden me, and to be **MYSELF**

Dear Karthick!

   You are in the world of creators who created three crores and still counting gods and goddesses. Man is creature who gained spirituality by relating the power to the stones. The same man is also a creature who brought spirituality within himself with his sagacious work.

120

Now it's time to believe in something to live for,
love for, fear for. Why on earth man doesn't
search logic to love for, but needs proof to pray
for?.

Believe in anything in this world until it doesn't
discomforts others and also you. Believe in your
fear, in your love, in your life, in your thoughts.
Believe in your words. It's after all, belief which
brought so many changes in this world.

You stood in between the bridge of childhood,
adulthood; Love and Death; Work and success;
End and Start.

Nothing, happened in your life goes in vain
without either teaching you or leaving you in
tatters.

You've lived where life took you to the extremes,
to the highs, to the lows, to the rags, to the riches,
to the love, to the death.

Past is part of you.
Either you can take it, learn from it or leave it,
living in it.

You've two options
1)Thinking about the past, crying for it and go wherever life takes.
2)Cherishing the past, smiling for the love& go where ever you want to have life.

Life is not a fairy tale to live in the fantasies. Life is also a journey, jostling you, to face the problems in reality.

Be passionate. Passion is to be in the mess. Passion is to love the mess you create.

Passion is not done perfunctorily. Passion is patters of thoughts not letting you sleep.

Passion makes you pallid, pangs you, puts you in peril. Passion makes you poised, pompous.

It's the passion which takes you, transforms you to be someone better than, who you were last day, last hour.

Passion is perception to make you the man of

perspectives & live in the process of achieving your dream.

Success is not what you achieve, it is ride undergone through hell and heaven.

Karthick

Being passionate about words, writings. I started writing about life, thoughts, feelings, fears. Months passed with writer blocks in my mind, but it's passion which I put up with, moved me forward, to be the man of perspectives.

Letter from Amu and from me, always fuelled me to dream what I want to be.

Darkness, brought me into the light, exposing me into the world of writers where,

ABHINAY RENNY

**No one is around
to ask, to talk**

**Tore up the tattered life
With the touch of darkness**

Darkness is my light of this night

**To search for "ME"
To recall "ME"**

Darkness is my torch on this night

**To drive away the dread
To make a new way, to be led**

**Stars decorated the darkness
With their limited sparks**

**Beautiful black sky
Blessed is this night!**

After then, becoming familiar, I could sense the
power of knowing, and being known where,

**Know more, to know, you know less
No more to, "NO" when you want to know
more**

**Knowing the value of being known
Do not forget to know the perks of being
unknown.**

4 years passed.

In the roller coaster ride of life. With whatever
intentions, I joined engineering, all are fulfilled
making me smile, cry, fear, love, and live.

And now, I'm crossing the bridge, from engineering
student to the Writer, Poet. In between the bridge
of life. Believing in myself.

Hard times are going to pang me, but can't win over
me.

From the times of watching interviews to kill time, I
spend now, time, giving interview on the occasion of
becoming renown writer at young age.

Interviewer: What do you want to become?

Karthick : Lover's husband

Interviewer: What did you become?

Karthick: Lover's son [laughs]

Interviewer: ?? explain please.

Karthick: I was, am, will be father's son! By now you should know who my lover is. He let me live, grow, fail, achieve, cry.

Interviewer: What did you learn from your engineering life?

Karthick :

"I am a student, learn after education that, "learning" is what I still didn't learn till now."

In between the bridge

**Like a flash
crossed the childhood**

**Was brat
whom everyone adore**

**had a gang to hang on
nothing to nag on**

**In between the bridge
of childhood and adulthood**

**A new view
of the world**

**Got only few
to share and care**

**In between the bridge of
adaptation and habitation**

**I'm a loner
chosen to choose it
sometimes, I love it**

I shut the world

to be in my world
dancing to the rhythm
enhancing the life

In between the bridge
of solitude and serenity

Crying to complete the incomplete
regret, is what I don't get it
Nothing at fullest
Not happy, not sad

In between the bridge
of fulfillment and contentment

I'm on a roller coaster ride
Rolling with problems
Riding the life

Crossing the bridges
to the distant destination

In between the bridge

EPILOGUE

Karthick is in the woods travelling to learn and learning to travel. Looking at him, My face turned all smiles, loving him, wishing him the best in his life.

I'm Amrutha in between the bridge of death and

I don't know why, but

Thank you Susmitha Gopi, Jishan, Bada a.k.a Bhargav.

ABOUT THE AUTHOR

T.Abhinay mostly called as Abhinay Renny is graduating in "MECHANICAL ENGINEERING" at VNR VJIET, Hyderabad.

Abhinay loves to spend time with his guitar and is an enthusiastic athlete. He believes in Individuality which saves the souls and also the world. He loves to pen down his thoughts in form of poems and letters to himself.

For more information on Abhinay, check him out on the websites below

Blog: Abhinayrenny.blogspot.in
Facebook:
https://www.facebook.com/authorabhinayrenny
Email : Abhinayrenny@gmail.com

IN BETWEEN THE BRIDGE

Inked Word

Check his poems on

Facebook : https://www.facebook.com/inkword